Christine Graham is the author of *Three Little Robbers*. She lives in an old house in Salt

husband

D0679516

Other chapter books you might enjoy

Boo's Dinosaur
Boo's Surprise
Betsy Byars, illustrated by Erik Brooks

Dragon Tooth Trouble
written and illustrated by Sarah Wilson

Fat Bat and Swoop
Sea Surprise
written and illustrated by Leo Landry

Lavender
Karen Hesse, illustrated by Andrew Glass

Little Horse
Little Horse on His Own
Betsy Byars, illustrated by David McPhail

Maybelle in the Soup
Maybelle Goes to Tea
Katie Speck, illustrated by Paul Rátz de Tagyos

Sable
Karen Hesse, illustrated by Marcia Sewall

SECOND-GRADE FRIENDS:

The Secret Lunch Special (Book 1)
No More Pumpkins (Book 2)
The Veterans Day Visitor (Book 3)
Peter Catalanotto and Pamela Schembri

Three Little Robbers
Christine Graham, illustrated by Susan Boase

Peter Peter Picks a Pumpkin House

Christine Graham

Illustrations by Susan Boase

Henry Holt and Company ❧ New York

Henry Holt and Company, LLC
Publishers since 1866
175 Fifth Avenue
New York, New York 10010
www.HenryHoltKids.com

Library of Congress Cataloging-in-Publication Data
Graham, Christine.
Peter Peter picks a pumpkin house / Christine Graham ; illustrations
by Susan Boase. — 1st ed.
p.   cm.
Summary: Peter Peter and his wife, Wanda, who grow pumpkins
in a field outside their little hut, find an unusual solution to the
problem of a leaky roof.
ISBN 978-0-8050-8706-2
[1. Pumpkin—Fiction.] I. Boase, Susan, ill. II. Title.
PZ7.G751673Pe 2009   [Fic]—dc22   2008049228

First Edition—2009 / Designed by Véronique Lefèvre Sweet
Printed in June 2009 in the United States of America by Worzalla,
Stevens Point, Wisconsin, on acid-free paper. ∞

1 3 5 7 9 10 8 6 4 2

To my parents, who taught me to love words
—C. G.

Thanks to my husband, Greg,
for his gardening genes
—S. B.

Contents

Peter Peter Picks a Pumpkin House

CHAPTER 1

Life Was Lovely

Every morning, when the sun lit the tops of the bingbang trees, Peter Peter got out his hoe. He stretched his arms and smiled.

"Another great day to hoe pumpkins," he said.

He went to the pumpkin field and
hoed away the weeds. He sang to the
pumpkin vines.

> *Grow, oh, grow,*
> *Oh, pumpkins so*
> *Big and round*
> *On the ground.*

Every morning, when the sun lit the
roots of the bingbang trees, Peter Peter's
wife, Wanda, got out her buckets. She
stretched her arms and smiled.

"Another great day to water pumpkins," she said.

She filled her buckets with water.
Then she put pumpkin muffins and a
bottle of goat milk in a basket. She went
to the pumpkin field.

She watered the pumpkins. She
shared goat milk and muffins with Peter
Peter.

"The vines thank you and I thank
you," said Peter Peter.

Every evening, when the sun set behind the bingbang trees, Peter Peter and Wanda sat on the porch of their hut. The hut was made of mud.

They drank red tea and watched their goat eat grass. They watched the pumpkins grow fat in the field.

"We have many pumpkins," said Peter Peter.

"I will make many muffins and pies," Wanda said.

"And cookies," said Peter Peter.

Peter Peter and Wanda watched the round orange sun set.

Life was lovely.

CHAPTER 2

The Rains

Life was not lovely when the rains came. The roof of the little hut dripped. Mud slopped onto the table. Mud plopped onto the bed.

Mud oozed between Wanda's toes. Mud glopped into Peter Peter's hair.

Peter Peter put pots and buckets on the floor to catch drips. Wanda stood under an umbrella to stir the pumpkin soup. The goat hid in the washtub.

"Rain makes me sad and soggy," said Wanda.

"But rain makes pumpkins grow round and fat," said Peter Peter. "Then the sun will come and make them orange."

"The sun cannot come too soon," said Wanda.

CHAPTER 3

A Visit

Wanda's father came for a visit. He soaked his tired feet in a bucketful of rain. Wanda fed him pumpkin pancakes.

"This hut is muddy," he said.

"Yes, because the roof is leaky," said Peter Peter. "Soon the pumpkins will grow fat and orange. We will sell some and get money for a new roof."

"Peter Peter, I worry," said Wanda's father. "You cannot wait for the pumpkins. Wanda will catch a cold in this drippy hut." He chewed his pancake slowly.

A drip from Wanda's umbrella
snaked down Peter Peter's back. Peter
Peter shivered. Then he looked out the
window and saw the goat. Peter Peter
smiled.

"Don't worry," he said. "Tomorrow I
will sell the goat, and I will buy tin to
fix the roof."

"I will go home," said Wanda's
father. "I want to get dry. But I will be
back soon."

He hugged Wanda good-bye. He put
on his shoes. He put up his umbrella
and slogged out into the rain.

CHAPTER 4

Treasure

The next morning when the sun lit the tops of the bingbang trees, Peter Peter put on his boots. He took the goat and started toward the village.

Clouds blew in. It began to rain again.
Peter Peter slipped in the mud. The goat
dripped and drooped.

"Who will buy such a sad, wet goat?"
thought Peter Peter.

An old, old man came down the
road. The old man's coat dragged. His
hat drooped. His nose dripped.

"Good day, sir," said Peter Peter.

"Good day it is not!" sniffled the old, old man. "The mud is so bad. I cannot get to the village to buy a goat."

"What luck!" said Peter Peter. "I have a goat to sell."

"Good," said the old, old man. "I will give you this bag of treasure. You will give me your goat."

Peter Peter looked at the big, lumpy
bag. It seemed like a lot of treasure.

"The goat is yours," said Peter Peter.
He took the bag and headed for the
village.

CHAPTER 5

The Wrong Treasure

Peter Peter went to the tin seller.

"Sir," he said. "Here is a big bag of treasure. I want tin to make a tight roof."

"What is this treasure?" asked the tin seller.

"Look and see," said Peter Peter.

The tin seller looked into the bag. "Ho ho! This is not treasure. These are big seeds!" he said.

"Ho ho!" said Peter Peter. "It must be the wrong bag. I will be back."

Peter Peter ran out the door and
down the road. He looked and looked.

He could not find the old, old man.
He could not find the goat. He slipped
in the mud and sat flat in a puddle.

When he got home, he threw the bag
of seeds into the mud. He jumped on it.

"I made a bad trade," he told Wanda.
"Your father will come back and find a
leaky roof."

All afternoon Peter Peter sat in the
muddy hut. He did not eat the muffins
Wanda baked. He was too sad.

"Don't worry," said Wanda.
"Something will come up."

"I hope so," said Peter Peter.

CHAPTER 6

Something Comes Up

That evening when the sun set behind the bingbang trees, Peter Peter and Wanda sat on the porch of their mud hut.

They watched the grass grow long. They watched the pumpkins get round.

"I miss the goat," said Wanda.

"I miss the goat milk," said Peter Peter.

Then a bump jumped up in the grass. Something green popped out. It was round and skinny. It wiggled and turned.

"A snake!" said Peter Peter. "Run, Wanda! Get into the hut!"

"It looks like a big sprout," said Wanda.

"Come in now!" yelled Peter Peter.

Wanda ran into the hut. Peter Peter locked the door and shut the window. Something outside thumped and bumped.

"What is bumping out there?" asked Wanda.

"I do not know," said Peter Peter, "but I am glad we are safe inside."

"So am I," said Wanda.

CHAPTER 7

A Big Surprise

The next morning, when the sun lit the tops of the bingbang trees, Peter Peter and Wanda were still snoring. The hut was dark.

Wanda woke up. The light in the hut was green.

She opened the window. A big leaf had grown over it.

She went out on the porch. A big vine had grown around it.

"It was not a snake, Peter Peter," said Wanda.

"It was a big sprout!" said Peter Peter.

He stretched his arms and smiled.
"What a great day to hoe a big vine!" he
said.

Peter Peter hoed the grass and weeds away from the big vine. Then he went to hoe the pumpkins.

When the sun lit the roots of the bingbang trees, Wanda got out her buckets.

"What a great day to water pumpkins," she said.

She filled her buckets with water. Then
she put pumpkin muffins in a basket. She
went to the field.

She watered the pumpkins. She
shared pumpkin muffins with Peter Peter.
Then she carried water to the big vine.

The vine grew and grew.

Every day Peter Peter and Wanda hoed and watered.

Every night as the sun set behind the bingbang trees, Peter Peter and Wanda sat on the porch of their little hut.

The leaves made the porch like a green cave.

"We cannot watch our pumpkins grow," said Wanda.

"But the big leaves keep out rain," said Peter Peter.

CHAPTER 8

A Big Pumpkin

One morning when the sun lit the roots of the bingbang trees, Peter Peter got out his hoe. He stretched his arms and smiled.

"What a great day to hoe pumpkins," he said. He walked out under the big vine. Then he stopped.

"Wanda!" he called. "There is a bud on the big vine."

Wanda came to see. "It is as big as your head, Peter Peter," said Wanda.

Soon more buds grew, and big blossoms opened. Then a round green pumpkin began to grow.

Peter Peter hoed the big vine and sang to it.

Grow, oh, grow,
Oh, pumpkin so
Big and round
On the ground.

The rain came. The pumpkin grew
round and fat and big.

It grew big as a washtub.

It grew big as a wagon.

It grew big as the hut.

CHAPTER 9

A New House

One evening, when the sun set behind the bingbang trees, Peter Peter and Wanda went out to look at the big pumpkin. It was orange and hard and huge.

"What will we do with this big
pumpkin?" asked Wanda. "It is as big
as a house."

Peter Peter smiled. "What a great
idea!" he said.

The next morning Peter Peter got his saw. He cut a door in the side of the pumpkin. Wanda looked in. "Ew!" she said. "This is a stringy, sticky house."

Peter Peter stretched his arms and smiled. "What a great day to clean house," he said.

He got out his hoe. He pulled out the big seeds and spread them in the sun to dry.

"These are treasure," he said. Then he pulled out the stringy stuff.

Wanda brought her buckets. Peter Peter and Wanda carried the stringy stuff away.

Then Peter Peter scraped the inside of the pumpkin clean. He left only a hard pumpkin shell.

Wanda took the pumpkin flesh. She made pumpkin pies.

Peter Peter cut windows. He built a porch.

"Come inside, Wanda," called Peter Peter from the pumpkin shell house.

"My goodness!" said Wanda. "What a wonderful orange house!"

CHAPTER 10

Pumpkin Pies

The next morning when the sun lit the tops of the bingbang trees, Peter Peter stretched his arms and smiled.

"What a great day for moving in," he said.

Wanda stretched her arms and smiled. "Yes. What a great day for moving in," she said.

They had pumpkin pie for breakfast. Then they moved into the pumpkin shell house.

Wanda's father came for a visit.

"Oh!" he said. "What a great orange house! What yummy pumpkin pies!"

"I am glad you are here," said Wanda. "I have a plan for these pies."

Peter Peter and Wanda's father helped carry pies to the village. Wanda sold pies all day.

When the sun was over the bingbang trees, there was one pie left. Wanda's father took it home.

Then Peter Peter and Wanda bought a goat. They took their goat home.

As the sun set behind the bingbang
trees, Peter Peter and Wanda sat on the
porch of their pumpkin shell house.
They drank red tea. They watched their
goat eat grass.

Life was lovely.